P9-DXN-073

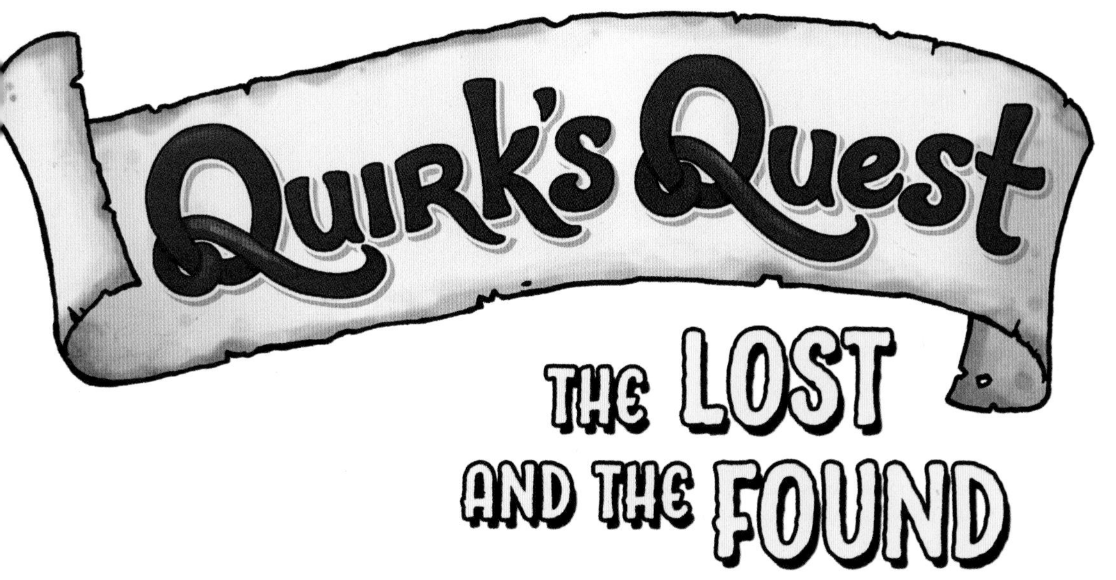

THE LOST AND THE FOUND

Robert Christie Deborah Lang

First Second
New York

Published by First Second
First Second is an imprint of Roaring Brook Press,
a division of Holtzbrinck Publishing Holdings Limited Partnership
175 Fifth Avenue, New York, NY 10010

Library of Congress Control Number: 2017946153

ISBN: 978-1-62672-234-7

Our books may be purchased in bulk for promotional, educational, or business use. Please contact your local bookseller or the Macmillan Corporate and Premium Sales Department at (800) 221-7945 ext. 5442 or by email at MacmillanSpecialMarkets@macmillan.com.

First edition, 2018

Book design by Rob Steen

Printed in China by Toppan Leefung Printing Ltd., Dongguan City, Guangdong Province

10 9 8 7 6 5 4 3 2 1

Drawn with 2H Sanford Turquoise pencils and inked with 03, 05, and 08 mm Micron pens on HP Premium Choice Laser Paper and Strathmore 400 Series Bristol Board. Colored digitally using Photoshop CC and a Wacom Intuos Pro tablet. Additional texture created with Dr. Ph. Martin's Synchromatic Transparent Watercolors on Strathmore 400 Series cold press watercolor paper. Nersel's maps hand-painted with FW acrylic ink and Windsor & Newton Artists' Watercolors using Princeton 0 and 2 watercolor brushes on Canson Montval cold press watercolor paper.

Quirk's Captain's Log, mission day 18
Merely eighteen days into our journey we have already experienced more harrowing ordeals than many do in a lifetime.
We have survived encounters with the monstrous Hooklm, albeit at the expense of our ship.
SMASH!
Finding shelter with the reclusive Hukka at first seemed most fortunate, but she proved a dangerous host, to say the least!
Our good luck returned once the Yoons of Lukki's Grotto took us in.

We lingered with them for a week, but finally our mission called, bringing us to our current encampment along the banks of a mighty stream that we have named the Maboоglaqui River. This is derived loosely from the Yoons' name for it, meaning "big swift."

WE'VE MADE OUTSTANDING PROGRESS THIS WEEK, BUT SOON WE WILL HAVE TO PRESS ON. WE NEED TO CROSS THE RIVER, AND SO I SHALL INSTRUCT GIMIL TO SCOUT AHEAD AND FIND A PROPER ROUTE.

AH, UM... CAPTAIN, SIR?
YES, GIMIL, WHAT IS IT?

UM, SIR, GEE, THERE'S THIS BIG CREATURE...

RRRROWWWAAAWWW!

WHAT WAS THAT?

WHY, THAT SOUNDS LIKE A ROXXANN, QUITE CLOSE, I SHOULD SAY...

SHALL WE TAKE A LOOK?

HE...HE WAS OVER BY THAT RIDGE!

OVER THERE!

HMM, YES! IT IS A ROXXANN. A BIG FELLOW, TOO.

PROBABLY A NORTHERN VARIETY ADAPTED TO THE HARSH CONDITIONS.
SHOULD WE BE CONCERNED?

I WOULD ADVISE A DOUBLE WATCH TONIGHT. ROXXANNS HAVE BEEN KNOWN TO GO INTO SETTLEMENTS AND DEVOUR FOLKS WHOLE.

REALLY? THAT IS QUITE HORRID!

OR MAYBE WE COULD... HMMM...

SNAP!

AAAAAAAHHH!!
BRRROXYANN!!

POUNCE!
SNAP!
SPROING!
AAAAAAAAHHH!!

RRRROXXYOWR!
EXCELLENT.

NEXT MORNING, THE SXERVIANS BUILT A PEN FOR THE NEWLY CAPTURED ROXXANN.
DON'T GIVE TOO MUCH SLACK— WE'LL CUT THE ROPE ONCE THE ENCLOSURE IS FINISHED.
AH, BURTRYM! I SEE YOUR PLAN WAS QUITE SUCCESSFUL!

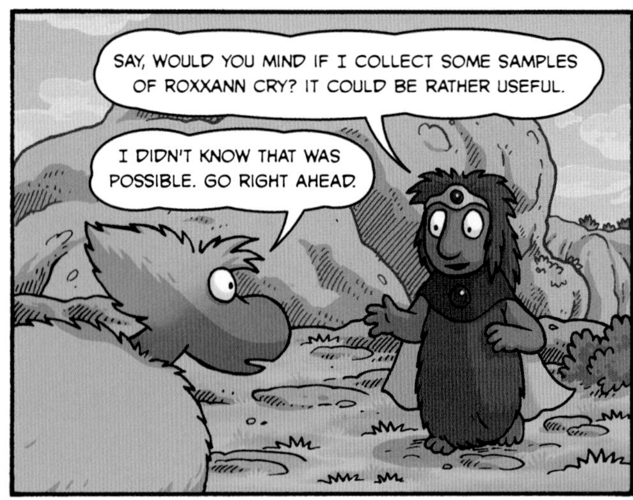
SAY, WOULD YOU MIND IF I COLLECT SOME SAMPLES OF ROXXANN CRY? IT COULD BE RATHER USEFUL.
I DIDN'T KNOW THAT WAS POSSIBLE. GO RIGHT AHEAD.

FANTASTIC. CLEUS, YOU MAY COLLECT THE SAMPLES— BE CAREFUL!

ALL RIGHT.

SNAP!

EASY NOW.
DRAW IT OUT...

NOT TOO CLOSE!
CAREFUL!

GOT IT!

OUTSTANDING. COLLECT A FEW MORE SAMPLES AND I WILL MEET YOU BACK IN CAMP.

CRASH!

SMOK! WHAT'S GOING ON HERE?
GO AWAY! KELDORN WILL GET YOU!

OH, HI, LANITEE... JUST GIVIN' THE PATIENT HIS BREAKFAST!

HE'S NOT TOO JOLLY THIS MORNIN', BUT AT LEAST HIS AIM WITH CROCKERY IS IMPROVIN'.

HEY, ZAIFER, YOU HAVE A VISITOR.
THIS CAMP IS FULL OF WORTHLESS IDIOTS!

I STRONGLY SUGGEST YOU CURB YOUR DEPLORABLE BEHAVIOR.

BUT PRIESTESS...I ONLY WENT ON THIS MISSION AS A MEANS OF PURSUING A HOLY QUEST FOR MY TRIBE...

...AND INSTEAD, OUR THICK-HEADED CAPTAIN AND HIS GANG OF IMBECILES STRAND US HERE! NOW I AM BROKEN AND USELESS.

HOW UNGRATEFUL! OTHERS HAVE SUFFERED WORSE THAN YOU, LIKE POOR SHELBY, WHO PERISHED IN YOUR RESCUE. YOU TAKE FOOD AND SHELTER WITHOUT ANY GRATITUDE.
BUT MY MISSION IS MORE IMPORTANT!

BUCHEBEEST'S BILE! NONE OF THE MEEMOO THAT I MET AT THE ROCK WERE SO SELFISH!

BUT PRIESTESS! YOU KNOW HOW SIGNIFICANT A MISSION FORESEEN BY A STORYTELLER IS...
OUR STORYTELLER HAD A VISION, AN OMEN, OF A DOUBLE-PEAKED MOUNTAIN IN THE OLD-LANDS.
I NEEDED TO GO NORTH AND SEEK THIS PLACE, FOR THE GOOD OF THE TRIBE...TO FULFILL THIS HOLY PROPHECY.
IN THE HEART OF THIS MOUNTAIN I WOULD FIND MY PROPER DESTINY.
MY ÔR WOULD BE WHOLE, AND THE TRIBE WOULD BE IN BALANCE.

IF YOU UNDERSTOOD THE MAIN CALLING OF THOSE WITHIN ZEEPINTOL ROCK, THEN YOU WOULD KNOW THAT WE HONOR NOT JUST YOUR MEEMOO BELIEFS, BUT THE JOURNEYS OF MANY CULTURES.
YES, PRIESTESS.

THEN YOU SEE THAT NO ONE'S MISSION HERE IS GREATER THAN THE WHOLE, NOT EVEN YOURS.

WHAT ARE YOU DOING?
UNNH...

ZAIFER! DON'T!
UFF!

YOU MUSTN'T EXERT YOURSELF!
UNGHH!

ZAIFER!
PLEASE! FORGIVE ME, HOLY PRIESTESS! I DID NOT KNOW MY PLACE.
FINE, FINE!

NOT AN IDEAL SITUATION, BUT AT LEAST THERE SHOULD BE LESS ATTITUDE.

ER, LANITEE, MA'AM?

YES, SMOK, WHAT IS IT?

WHY'D ZAIFER TREAT YA LIKE THAT? ALL RESPECTFUL. NOT A BAD THING, BUT IT'S NOT LIKE HIM OR NOTHIN'.

IT IS BECAUSE I AM A ZEEP. DO YOU KNOW ABOUT ZEEP, SMOK?

NO, MA'AM.

ALL OF US ZEEP LIVE IN ZEEPINTOL ROCK, WITHIN THE MOST REMOTE AND DESOLATE PART OF THE WAAXYE DESERT. OUR CULTURE IS CENTERED ON LEARNING, SPIRITUAL GUIDANCE, AND MYSTICISM. MANY CULTURES MAKE PILGRIMAGES TO THE ROCK TO SEEK THE COUNSELING OF THE ZEEP PRIESTESSES.

MEEMOO ARE REGULAR VISITORS, BUT THEIR BELIEFS ARE A BIT DIFFERENT THAN THAT OF MANY CRUTONIANS...

THE MAJORITY OF CRUTONIANS BELIEVE THAT THE NATURAL WORLD IS SUFFUSED IN A KIND OF DIVINE MAGIC.

AND WHAT DO THE MEEMOO BELIEVE?
MEEMOO TAKE THE DIVINE ASPECT AND GIVE IT DISTINCT PERSONALITIES. THEY BELIEVE THAT THE NATURAL FORCES ARE CONTROLLED BY GODS.

CHYZYKARA, THE ALL-SEEING DEITY OF TRUTH AND THE SUNS.

EL-HET-HET-WETEN, LORD OF TRICKERY, THE MOON, AND THE NORTH; MASTER OF FOG AND THE CLOUDS.

KELDORN, GOD OF THUNDER, VENGEANCE, AND PUNISHMENT.

ZNX, WHOSE DOMINION IS THE EARTH AND ALL LIVING THINGS.

TZWA, GOD OF WATER AND PEACE.

THE WILLS OF THESE GODS ARE INTERPRETED BY THE TRIBAL LEADERS. EACH TRIBE HAS THREE CHIEF POSITIONS...

A MATRIARCH, CHOSEN BY OMEN.
A STORYTELLER, WHO MAINTAINS THE TRIBE'S HISTORY THROUGH STORY-SONGS.
AND A SEER, WHO STUDIES AND INTERPRETS THE OMENS.

IT IS MOST OFTEN THAT THESE SEERS VISIT US AT ZEEPINTOL ROCK TO SEEK ADVICE AND DEBATE THE MEANING OF VARIOUS OMENS.

THIS CAN LEAD TO SOME VERY INTERESTING PHILOSOPHICAL DISCUSSIONS...

WE ZEEP TRY TO BRING INSIGHT TO THE MEEMOO'S UNUSUAL WAY OF LOOKING AT THE WORLD. DO YOU UNDERSTAND?

NOT REALLY.

SO WHY DID YOU COME ON THIS MISSION, IF YOU ALREADY KNOW SO MUCH?
ACTUALLY, WE ZEEP RARELY LEAVE OUR HOME, BUT I HAVE LEARNED SO MUCH HERE IN THE OUTLANDS, MORE THAN MANY VOLUMES OF BOOKS.

RRRRRRR

AH, BURTRYM! I WAS WONDERING IF YOU STILL NEEDED MY BRIGADE OF FROGS?

THE SXERVIANS ARE JUST PUTTING THE FINISHING TOUCHES ON THE PEN NOW.
AH, GOOD. YOU SEE, I WOULD LIKE TO DO A BIT MORE SURVEYING... IT APPEARS THE TERRAIN IS ABOUT TO BECOME MORE ***DANGEROUS.***

DANGEROUS? WELL, HAVING THIS PEN ALLOWS FOR CLOSE OBSERVATION WITH SIGNIFICANTLY ***LESS RISK.***
OH, BUT IT ***WILL BE RISKY***. TREACHEROUS, EVEN! THERE ARE HUGE CLIFFS UPSTREAM THAT WE SHALL HAVE TO PLAN A ***HUGE*** DETOUR TO AVOID.

HUGE MIGHT BE AN OVERSTATEMENT, BUT THIS FELLOW IS NEARLY TWICE THE SIZE OF HIS SOUTHERN COUSINS.

SOUTHERN? YES, I SUPPOSE WE COULD HEAD SOUTH, BUT I AM RELATIVELY CERTAIN THAT IN THAT DIRECTION OUR OBSTACLES SHALL ONLY BECOME LARGER.

YES, MUCH LARGER! THEY LAY THEIR EGGS IN THE NESTS OF OTHER CREATURES, AND THE VICIOUS LITTLE HATCHLINGS DEVOUR THEIR NESTMATES, PERHAPS EVEN THE PARENT.

NO, IT'S NOT APPARENT THAT ONE CHOICE IS BETTER THAN THE ALTERNATIVE... THOUGH MY INSTINCT IS TO CONTINUE FOLLOWING THE RIVER...

...EXCUSE ME, GENTLEMEN, I MUST SEE WHAT THE CAPTAIN HAS TO SAY ABOUT ALL OF THIS.

WALDEMAR, ARE YOU GETTING ALL OF THIS?

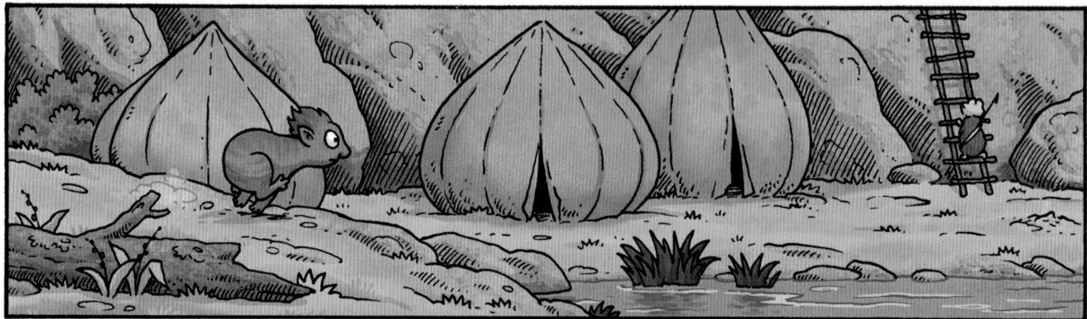

SIR!
SIR!
THERE IS SORTA—WELL, A HOUSE UP THE RIVER!

REALLY? WE SHOULD INVESTIGATE IT IMMEDIATELY.

WELL, IT LOOKS SAFE ENOUGH. SMOK—YOU AND GIMIL COME WITH ME.

HAVE THE CRIMSON BRIGADE FOLLOW AT A DISTANCE. THE AQUA BRIGADE WILL REMAIN HIDDEN UNTIL THERE IS A NEED.

M-MAYBE NO ONE'S HOME.

ONE MORE TIME.

HOLD ON, DEARS, I'LL BE RIGHT THERE!
KNOCK
KNOCK

HELLO, HELLO! VISITORS, HOW NICE!
AAAAHH!!
YIPES!
EEP!

ANOTHA HUKKA! LET'S GIT HER!

H-H-HUKKA! WE'RE SORRY!!
WE DIDN'T—WE THOUGHT—

HUKKA? GOODNESS NO!
I'M HER SISTER, XULDA.

HAAAARRRRR!!
OH, MY! WHAT'S ALL OF THIS ABOUT NOW?

WELL, NO MATTER. EASILY REMEDIED.
NOOO!!

THERE! NOW WHAT WERE YOU SAYING?

WHAT HAVE YOU DONE TO MY FROGS?

OH, DEARY, NO HARM DONE! JUST AN INTOXICATION SPELL... IT WILL WEAR OFF IN A JIFFY. LET ME MAKE IT UP TO YOU, MASTER QUIRK. I SHALL WHIP YOU UP A NICE HOT SUPPER.
HOW...HOW DO YOU KNOW US?

OH, I'VE HEARD ALL ABOUT YOU, SWEETIE, AND I AM SURE A GOOD MEAL IS WHAT YOU NEED. BRING ALONG SOME OF YOUR LITTLE FRIENDS, THREE AND THREE.

SEE YOU LATER! I'D BEST START COOKING.
GIVE AN OLD GIRL A CHANCE TO SPRUCE UP HER HAIRSTYLE, HEE HEE!

Quirk's Captain's Log, mission day 19

It is with some hesitancy that I prepare for our social visit with Xulda. Compounding what I hope to be a totally unsubstantiated suspicion of Xulda's intentions, I also bear the unpleasant news about her sister, Hukka.

While on task, Nersel and the Fuchsia Brigade continue to chart this wild terrain. Gimil is proving her scouting expertise in this endeavor.

AH, GIMIL. WE NEED TO DISCOVER AN OPTIMAL RIVER CROSSING POINT. SCOUT AHEAD AND SEE IF THERE IS ONE, WOULD YOU?
UM, YEAH, OKAY!

I leave brave Gnonek in charge of camp during my absence. He will coordinate a hunt for meats—the Poorkon are plentiful here and will provide adequate sustenance for our many Frogs. He will retain the Crimson and Aqua Brigades for this purpose and to guard our captive Roxxann.

WHUMP!

RRRROXYAWRR!!

For Xulda's banquet, my entourage includes Smok, Lanitee, Cleus, Burtrym, and inevitably of course, Waldemar. The Amber Brigade shall escort us, but due to the Sxervians' lack of natural social graces, shall remain outside of Xulda's abode.

ENJOY YOURSELVES, BUT LET CAUTION AND READINESS BE YOUR COMPANIONS.

COME ON IN, SWEETIES! FIND A CHAIR AND MAKE YOURSELVES COMFORTABLE.

THIS WAY... RIGHT THROUGH HERE.

WE MAY NOT HAVE THE INGREDIENTS THAT YOU ARE ACCUSTOMED TO, CAPTAIN, BUT I ASSURE YOU THAT IT IS GOURMET.

MADAM, I MUST INSIST THAT YOU REVEAL HOW YOU KNOW OF ME AND MY EXPEDITION.

I THINK HE SHOULD TELL YOU HIMSELF.
CAPTAIN...

SMOKES!

SORRILLIUS! YOU'RE ALIVE!
YES, IT IS I, SORRILLIUS, WHOM YOU LEFT FOR DEAD; LIFELESS...LIKE A HOLLOW WHISPER... SHALLOW IN THE GRAVE.

THIS IS A MIRACLE! WE THOUGHT YOU WERE DEVOURED BY THE HOOKLM!

AND YET I LIVE.

SORRILLIUS HAS PREPARED A LOVELY FEAST FOR YOU. PLEASE FIND A SEAT AND RELAX. SORRILLIUS CAN TELL YOU HIS TALE WHILE I FETCH THE MEAL.
MY TALE, AWASH WITH TRIAL AND HORROR! BUT TELL IT I MUST.

AFORE THE SHIPWRECK, IGNORANT AND UNPREPARED I WAS TO FATE, BOTH DREADFUL AND FORTUITOUS. OUTFITTED WITH ONLY THE FINEST STILTS TO ATTAIN A BETTER STATURE. FINE STILTS, HAND-CRAFTED EBRHVILLIAN-TAMBOO STICKS, TOUGH EXTERIOR BUT HOLLOW WITHIN.
YET THE HOOKLM CREATURES DETERMINED ME CANAPÉ. THE COOK NOW THE CUISINE.

SWALLOWED FOR SURE IF NOT FOR MY STILT; CHOKED THE BEAST AND RETURNED ME ONCE MORE TO THE REALM OF THE UNEATEN.

MY OTHER STILT 'TWAS STRAW FOR ME, AND I WAS ABLE TO REMAIN UNSEEN AND UNDIGESTED BENEATH THE BRINY DEPTHS.

I LEFT THE OCEAN'S FEARFUL EMBRACE WHERE SHE JOINED WITH THIS MIGHTY RIVER'S CONFLUENCE AND FOLLOWED ITS TUMULTUOUS TORRENTS ON INTO THESE CRAGGY HILLS.

IT WAS THENCE THAT I HAPPENED UPON A VISION SUBLIME, XULDA, GATHERING DYE-YIELDING HIKSL BERRIES. SHE IS AN EXQUISITE WEAVER... EXQUISITE IN MANY WAYS.

AND THAT IS WHERE MY SAGA CONCLUDES, HERE IN XULDA'S WARMEST HOSPITALITY.

THAT'S GREAT.
WHAT SORT OF PLANT IS THIS VEGETABLE FROM?

IT'S A GLYPTUM TUBER, AND SORRILLIUS HAS THRICE-BAKED IT TO CREATE THIS MOST SAVORY DISH.

REMARKABLE! AND DELICIOUS! CLEUS, WE MUST COLLECT SOME SPECIMENS.
SURE, BOSS.

OH! AND HOW DID YOU GET THE POORKON SO TENDER? MINE ALWAYS TURNS OUT STRINGY.

I WOULD SPECULATE THAT IS BECAUSE YOU BELONG IN THE SCULLERY, NOT THE KITCHEN.

BUT CAPTAIN, TELL ME, HOW IS IT YOU MANAGED TO EMERGE FROM OUR MARITIME MISHAP WITH AS MANY SOULS THIS SIDE OF A WATERY GRAVE?

WELL, MY DEAR FELLOW, WE WERE QUITE FORTUNATE, ACTUALLY.
LANITEE AND CLEUS HERE WERE ABLE TO LOCATE A CAVE WHERE WE COULD TAKE REFUGE FROM THOSE HORRIFYING MONSTERS.

WE LATER DISCOVERED THAT THE CAVE WAS HOME TO HUKKA AND, UH...

ALTHOUGH WE GOT OFF TO...AH, A BIT OF A ROCKY START, WE, UM...

OH, HUKKA... YOU MUST FORGIVE HER. SHE CAN BE QUITE IMPOSSIBLE SOMETIMES.

WELL, UH, YES, SHE ALLOWED US TO LINGER FOR A FEW DAYS, BUT THEN WE, UH, DECIDED TO SET UP A NEW CAMP IN A NEARBY AREA.
HEY! DON' FERGIT ABOUT THE YOONS! WE STAYED WITH THESE LI'L CRITTERS...

SMOK! I BELIEVE I WAS RECOUNTING THIS TALE.

OH, UH, SORRY, CAPT'N SIR! I JUST...

AS I WAS SAYING...WE SUBSEQUENTLY MET A LOCAL TRIBE OF CREATURES WHO CALLED THEMSELVES YOONS.

OH! SO YOU MET THE YOONS OF THE GROTTO. THAT MUST HAVE PUT HUKKA IN QUITE A STATE! SHE'S NOT VERY FOND OF THEM, I'M AFRAID.

THEY TREATED US VERY WELL AND WERE ABLE TO TEACH US SOMETHING OF THEIR WAYS. ISN'T THAT RIGHT, BURTRYM?

HMM? OH, YES, FASCINATING LITTLE, AH, CREATURES.
THEY'RE UNFLAME-ABLE!

YES...APPARENTLY. WELL, ANYWAY... WE SPENT A WEEK IN THE GROTTO, THEN MOVED ON YESTERDAY. WE ARE CAMPED JUST DOWNSTREAM FROM HERE. OUR SCOUT GIMIL DISCOVERED YOUR HOUSE.

NOW FOR DESSERT... SMOK! CLEAR THE DISHES!
CLAP! CLAP!

YESSIR!

XULDA, I WAS WONDERING IF I MIGHT HAVE A WORD WITH YOU IN PRIVATE.

OF COURSE, DEAR! RIGHT THROUGH HERE.

YOU LOOK WORRIED. NOW WHAT IS IT?
XULDA, I AM...SORRY TO SAY THAT I...I COME WITH SAD, SAD NEWS.

WHATEVER COULD YOU MEAN, MY DEAR?

UM, WELL, YOU SEE, WHEN WE WERE LEAVING HUKKA'S CAVES, THERE WAS AN ACCIDENT... I'M AFRAID A PART OF THE CAVE COLLAPSED.
OH, MY!

I DON'T THINK HUKKA SURVIVED...

WHAT? OH, NONSENSE, DEAR! IF ANYTHING REALLY BAD HAD HAPPENED TO HUKKA I WOULD SURELY KNOW.

YOU SEE MY TALISMAN? WE BOTH WEAR THEM. THEY ALLOW US TO COMMUNICATE. HERE, LET ME SHOW YOU...

UMMM...

MALABOO BARPEE PHAKO UST HUKKA LAX!

GREETINGS, DEAREST SISTER!

YOU! WHAT IS IT YOU WANT? OR ARE YOU JUST SPYING ON POOR HUKKA?
OH, I'M JUST CHECKING ON YOU, MAKING SURE YOU ARE ALL RIGHT. I HEARD THERE WAS A CAVE-IN.

WHO TOLD YOU THAT? YOU HAVE BEEN SPYING ON ME!
NOT AT ALL, DEAR SISTER, BUT I'VE MET SOME MOST INTERESTING FOLKS WHO CLAIM THEY STAYED WITH YOU, AND THEY SAID...

WHAT?! WHO IS IT? IS IT THAT SNEAKING, THIEVING QUIRK AND HIS WRETCHED BAND OF SCOUNDRELS? IT IS, ISN'T IT?

THIEVING? I CAN'T IMAGINE WHAT YOU ARE TALKING ABOUT, HUKKA. QUIRK AND HIS CREW ARE MOST...

IT *IS* THEM! THEY THERE WITH YOU NOW?! I MUST STOP THEM! I'LL BE RIGHT THERE!

BLAM!

OOH, SHE'S QUITE UPSET. IS THERE SOMETHING YOU FAILED TO TELL ME?
IT REALLY WASN'T OUR FAULT! WE DIDN'T KNOW, THEN SHE KIDNAPPED ONE OF OUR SCOUTS...

AHA! THEY ARE HERE!
AAH!!

THESE VILLAINS ROBBED ME OF MY SWEET HEKPA! THEY MUST PAY!!!
NO! HUKKA, PLEASE!

HEKPA?! ZNX PRESERVE US! WHAT IS THIS ALL ABOUT?

DON'T DEFEND THEM! ARE YOU MY SISTER OR NOT? WHERE DO YOUR LOYALTIES LIE?
OH, HUKKA! DON'T BE ABSURD! BUT SURELY THIS HEKPA BUSINESS HAS GONE ON LONG ENOUGH!

YESSS... I SEE NOW... YOU WERE JEALOUS OF MY HAPPINESS...
...OF MY SWEET HEKPA! AND IT IS YOU WHO MUST PAY!
ZORCH!!
NO! STOP THIS NONSENSE!
GAH!
ZOMPH!
CRASH!

WHERE IS HEKPA? GIVE HIM BACK TO ME!
NO! IT WASN'T HEKPA! IT WAS JUST MY SCOUT!

LIAR!

ZORCH!

YOU'VE KILLED HER!

PISH POSH! NO, DEARY, JUST ANOTHER INTOXICATION SPELL.

WE SHALL JUST GIVE HER SOME TIME TO REST.

LET'S ALL GO TO THE GARDEN, THEN? QUICK AND QUIET!

SO, NOBLE CAPTAIN, WHAT IS THIS ABOUT YOUR SCOUT?

OUR MEMOO SCOUT, ZAIFER, WAS INJURED DURING OUR, AH, MISHAP. HUKKA ERRONEOUSLY BELIEVES HIM TO BE SOMEONE NAMED HEKPA...

A WINGED MEEMO, THEN? JEEBISH MELONS!

WHO *IS* HEKPA?

SAKES! FORGET HEKPA! THERE IS NO HEKPA!
HUKKA...SHE HAS A WOUND IN HER HEART NONE CAN HEAL.

LEAVE ME BE, FROG.

CLEVER HUKKA, DECEPTIVE MIST THAT HIDES DECEIT FROM XULDA IS CLEAR TO YOU...

SPEAK NOT IN RIDDLES!

THE CAPTAIN THAT EXPLOITS XULDA'S KIND HOSPITALITY IS AS YOU SEE—CHARLATAN, INEPT...LIAR.
VILLAIN! BUT WHY REVEAL THIS TO HUKKA?!

I, TOO, A BLAMELESS VICTIM, LOYAL TO HIM, AND HE LEFT ME A CORPSE.

THEIR CAMP IS JUST TWO SKIPS DOWN RIVER.

DECEITFUL QUIRK! IGNORANT XULDA! EVIL, WICKED ZUPPA!

SWEET, SWEET...HEKPA!

KABLAM!

SNIFF
SNIFF

SWEET...
SWEET...

HEKPA!!
AAAAHHH!!

BOOMPH

HUH
HUH

WHY?!?

PLEASE, NO!
KLINK

SMASH!

AAARGGHH!
RRRRRROXHAAAAAAAAAARAAAAAAAAANNNN
AARGGH! MY EARS!
WHO DEAFENS HUKKA?

BONK

RRROW!!

AAAAHH!

EATON!

ZORCH!
FROGGIES! ATTACK!!

GAH!

KA-BLAM!
NOW *EVERYONE* WILL PAY!
...SEE, GIMIL, WE HAVE BEEN ABLE TO MAP THE SOUTH RIVER BANK UP TO THIS SECOND TRIBUTARY.
PERHAPS WE CAN CONVINCE THE CAPTAIN TO GIVE US A BIT MORE TIME, JUST TO EXPLORE THIS AREA OVER HERE...

ACH! WATCH IT!

THIS IS QUITE UNACCEPTABLE!

MARK MY WORDS, THE CAPTAIN WILL HEAR OF THIS!

MADNESS! HUKKA? IS THAT YOU?
BLAM!

HUKKA CANNOT HEAR YOUR PLEAS FOR MERCY!
ZORCH!

XULDA, HOW LONG BEFORE YOUR SISTER AWAKENS?
NOT MUCH LONGER. I SHOULD PROBABLY GO AND CHECK ON HER.

HUKKA?

YOU WON'T FIND HER... SHE IS VANISHED, A WISP OF SMOKE, A LINGERING AROMA OF VENGEANCE.

WHAT? GONE? I MUST WARN QUIRK!
COME, XULDA, THIS IS NOT YOUR CONCERN.

NO! YOU DO NOT UNDERSTAND. THIS RUNS MUCH DEEPER. SHE IS UNWELL. I MUST GO.

A SHORT WHILE LATER, BACK AT CAMP...

SCURRYING SKABBEES! GNONEK, WHAT HAPPENED HERE?!

IT WAS HUKKA, SIR! MADDER THAN A MOOKIE'S MOTHER!

IS EVERYONE ALL RIGHT?

UNFORTUNATELY, NO.

ZAIFER!?

NAW, HE'S FINE. CAN'T HEAR NOTHIN' BUT HE'S ALL RIGHT... IT WAS THE FROGGIE NAMED EATON. THE ROXXANN GOT 'IM.

AND WHAT HAVE YOU DONE TO MY ROXXANN?! YOU FROGS WILL PAY FOR THIS!

BURTRYM! THERE ARE MORE IMPORTANT THINGS RIGHT NOW!

HUMPH!

I CAN SEE HUKKA HAS REMOVED HER AMULET.
IT IS IN A PLACE I HAVEN'T BEEN IN MANY YEARS.
I FEAR YOU ARE ALL IN GRAVE DANGER.

YOU SHOULD BE ON YOUR WAY, AND QUICKLY!
BUT IT IS GETTING DARK, AND WE DO NOT KNOW OUR WAY IN THESE LANDS. WE MUST STAY UNTIL MORNING.

KNOWING HER, I DON'T BELIEVE SHE WILL BE BACK THIS NIGHT, BUT I WILL STAY JUST IN CASE. YOU SHOULD SET A FULL WATCH.

DESPITE XULDA'S MISGIVINGS, THE NIGHT PASSED UNEVENTFULLY.

XULDA, SINCE YOU KNOW THE REGION, I WILL DEFER TO YOU AS TO OUR NEXT MOVE.

I WOULD SUGGEST YOU CROSS THE RIVER AT MY HOUSE AND HEAD DUE WEST... THE AREA TO THE SOUTH IS NOT SAFE FOR REASONS I'M NOT AT LIBERTY TO DISCUSS.

FINE. WE SHALL PICK UP SORRILLIUS ON OUR WAY.

SMOK, HAVE THE SXERVIANS PACK UP... WE WILL DEPART AS SOON AS POSSIBLE!

XULDA, YOU SPOKE OF DANGER TO THE SOUTH. MAY I REMIND YOU I AM AN EMISSARY OF HIS MAJESTY. I NEED TO KNOW IF THIS IS A THREAT TO THE REALM.

THREAT TO THE REALM? GOODNESS NO! IT IS A PRIVATE MATTER BETWEEN MY SISTER, MYSELF, AND A LOCAL TRIBE.

AS I SAID, I AM NOT AT LIBERTY TO DISCUSS IT. IT IS ENOUGH TO SAY THAT YOU WOULD BE WISE TO STAY CLEAR OF IT.

BUT ENOUGH ABOUT ME, DEAR. WHAT ABOUT YOU? HOW DID YOU FIND YOURSELF LEADING THIS EXPEDITION?

HIS MAJESTY, IN HIS WISDOM, SEES THE VALUE IN EXPLORATION AND ONLY APPOINTS THE MOST WORTHY OF LEADERS.

DURING THE WAR, I SERVED AS AN OFFICER FOR THE CROWN.
IT WAS MY FIRST COMMISSION.

YES, YES. WE CHASED THE ERBIAN FOREIGNERS OUT OF OUR LANDS...

AND THE LAST OF THE SCHLORGKS ARE FINALLY GONE.

WE OVERCAME THESE INVADERS DUE TO THE CLEVERNESS OF MYSELF AND THE OTHER OFFICERS.

WE WERE VICTORIOUS DUE TO OUR HARD WORK AND SHEER DETERMINATION.

FOR THIS, I WAS HONORED BY OUR KING HOONKL.
IT WAS THESE FIRST EXPERIENCES THAT EMPHASIZED MY INNATE APTITUDE FOR LEADERSHIP AND THE NATURAL ADMIRATION I GARNER FROM THOSE I COMMAND.

ARK!
ARK!

WHAT IS IT, ARKARK? HMM?

JUST SOME BREEZE IN THE BUSHES. C'MERE.

NOTHIN' TO GET UPSET ABOUT.
RRRRRR

SKREEEF!!

WHAT THE FRIGGLE WAS THAT?

IT SEEMS WE HAVE ATTRACTED THE ATTENTION OF SOME SNARLOX.

WHAT YOU HEAR IS A GROUP OF FEMALES OUT HUNTING... THERE WILL BE A DEN NEARBY, HARBORING A MUCH LARGER, BUT FAR MORE DOCILE, MALE AND A CLUTCH OF THEIR OFFSPRING.

THEY MIGHT JUST BE WARNING US TO STAY CLEAR OF THEIR DEN, BUT ON THE OTHER HAND, THEY MIGHT SEE US AS POTENTIAL MEALS.

BURTRYM, MAKE SURE YOU DO A COMPLETE STUDY ON THESE SNARLOX CREATURES...

WE MUSTN'T—

WHAT'S THIS? WHAT IS GOING ON HERE?

IT'S BAD...
VERY BAD.

XULDA, I INSIST YOU TELL ME WHAT THIS IS ALL ABOUT.

NO, THE LESS YOU KNOW, THE BETTER.

YOU AND YOUR PARTY NEED TO COME WITH US.

SEE HERE! I AM AN EMISSARY FROM THE KING!

YOU AND YOUR KING HAVE NO AUTHORITY HERE, QUIRK.

YOU ARE OUTNUMBERED... NOW LET US PASS!

THWAK

COME. WE DO NOT WISH TO HARM YOU.

HOW CAN YOU SAY THAT?! YOU JUST KILLED SCHMITS!

THEY ARE INNOCENT! THEY KNOW NOTHING!

XULDA, YOU KNOW OUR LAWS.

PIOUS FOLLOWERS OF KELDORN,
SEE BEFORE YOU XULDA THE BETRAYER...
...AND THOSE SHE HAS LED TO US.

GASP THE LOST
TRIBE OF KELDORRA!

WE ARE ON AN
OFFICIAL TOUR UNDER
THE AUSPICES OF OUR
ROYAL HIGHNESS, THE
KING OF CRUTONIA!
YOUR TREATMENT OF US
IS MOST DISHONORABLE.

WE HONOR YOU MORE THAN YOU DESERVE.

WHO ARE YOU TO QUESTION THE WILL OF A GOD?

HEY!
COME ALONG, PRIESTESS.

BE CAREFUL, CAPTAIN! THEY WILL BE TESTING YOU!

BY ORDER OF THE CROWN, I DEMAND AN EXPLANATION!
HAVEN'T YOU ALREADY HAD YOUR EXPLANATION? XULDA MUST HAVE BEEN VERY INFORMATIVE.

NO! I TOLD THEM NOTHING!

XULDA, YOU MAY JOIN YOUR SISTER IN UP-CHAMBERS.
SPLEENIK, LOCK THE REST IN THE ROOT CELLAR FOR NOW.

WAIT, WAIT! WHY WON'T YOU LISTEN?

VERY WELL. I WILL MEET WITH YOU TOMORROW. THE NEW DAY WILL BRING THE CLARITY OF REST AND WISDOM.

UNTIL THEN, I SUGGEST YOU TRY TO FIND COUNSEL AND COMFORT FROM WHATEVER GODS YOU HONOR.

IN YOU GO.

YOU'LL STAY HERE TONIGHT. DON'T EVEN THINK OF LEAVING THIS ROOM.

SLAM!

ROTS! WELL, AT LEAST THOSE GUARDS ARE FINALLY GONE.

CLEUS, TELL ME ABOUT THIS "LOST TRIBE OF KELDORRA."

I DON'T KNOW.

WHY NOT? LANITEE SEEMS TO KNOW.

SHE IS WELL READ IN MEEMOO CULTURE.
YES, YES. AS A ZEEP PRIESTESS, LANITEE MUST BE VERY KNOWLEDGEABLE IN MANY AREAS.

I AM WELL AWARE OF HER EXPERTISE, BURTRYM. WHAT ABOUT YOU?

AS OUR CULTURAL ANTHROPOLOGIST, SURELY YOU KNOW SOMETHING ABOUT THESE KELDORRANS?

WELL, THEY ARE A TRIBE OF MEEMOO, BUT FOR SOME REASON DON'T HAVE WINGS. THEY ALSO LIVE INSIDE A MOUNTAIN, INSTEAD OF ON TOP OF ONE. MOST ODD.

I MEANT ANYTHING NOT OBVIOUS.

HMMM... SO WE KNOW THEY ARE LOST SOMEHOW...

WELL, WE HAVE UNTIL MORNING TO THINK OF A PLAN.

PLACE THE FELLOW HERE.
WHO'S THIS?

HE'S A MEEMOO FROM THE OUTSIDE.
OH! A WINGED MEEMOO?

I'M PYNCHYN. KORAZON'S MY BROTHER.

WHERE ARE YOU FROM?
WHAT ARE YOU DOING HERE?
MOAN

PYNCHYN, HE NEEDS HIS REST.

PLEASE, DO YOU HAVE SOME HALBARK? MY EARS ARE RINGING... I HURT ALL OVER.

MEDICINALS, EH? I DON'T KNOW THIS HALBARK, BUT PYNCHYN CAN PREPARE YOU SOME JOJIG TEA AND KEDEROOT.

YES! I WILL TAKE CARE OF YOU!

ALL RIGHT. I HAVE TO REPORT TO JANKOO. REMEMBER, LET HIM REST.

PRIESTESS, THE TRIBUNE WILL NOT PASS JUDGMENT UNTIL TOMORROW. OUR SEER, KESTA-NA, INVITES YOU TO HER PRIVATE QUARTERS FOR A MEAL.

HOW ABOUT THE REST OF MY COMPANIONS?

I ONLY KNOW OUR SEER WISHES TO SPEAK TO YOU PERSONALLY.

WELL, AT LEAST LET ME HAVE MY ASSISTANT, CLEUS. HE IS AN UBR.

PLEASE, PRIESTESS, DO NOT BE ANGRY WITH ME. I ONLY SERVE KELDORN'S WILL... THIS WAY PLEASE.

I WILL GO FETCH THIS UBR. I BEG YOUR PATIENCE.

CLICK

YOU, THERE. YOUR ZEEP PRIESTESS REQUESTS HER ASSISTANT, AN UBR. IS THAT YOU?

UH, OH... YEAH. YEAH, SURE!

COME WITH ME.
GLADLY!

WHAT!? WAIT! GIMIL!!

SO YOU SEE, PRIESTESS, OUR SACRED TEMPLE IS WELL EQUIPPED WITH ANYTHING YOU MIGHT NEED.

AH, YOUR ASSISTANT HAS JOINED US.

PLEASE, MAKE YOURSELVES COMFORTABLE.
WE HAVE PREPARED A MEAL FOR YOU.

I AM SO HONORED BY YOUR PRESENCE. I NEVER IMAGINED I WOULD HAVE THE OPPORTUNITY TO SPEAK WITH ONE OF YOUR KIND.

I WILL FIND IT DIFFICULT TO PROVIDE ANY USEFUL COUNSEL WHILE MY CAPTAIN AND CREW ARE IN DANGER.

YES, YOUR CAPTAIN... I'M AFRAID I AM NOT IMPRESSED. HE IS QUITE HOSTILE.

HE MAY NOT BE PERFECT, BUT HE'S A GOOD CAPTAIN. YOU DISMISS HIM TOO QUICKLY.

HMM... SO HOW IS IT THAT A ZEEP PRIESTESS IS ON THIS MISSION?

WHY I AM HERE IS NOT REALLY THE IMPORTANT ISSUE RIGHT NOW.
I'M JUST SURPRISED TO FIND THAT SOMEONE OF YOUR BACKGROUND IS ASSOCIATED WITH THIS QUIRK FELLOW.

I FIND YOUR BLATANT DISRESPECT OF THE CAPTAIN QUITE UNJUSTIFIED.

HMM. WHAT ABOUT YOU, LITTLE ONE? WHAT DO YOU THINK OF YOUR CAPTAIN?

HUNH? WHAT? GEE, WELL... I THINK THE CAPTAIN IS THE GREATEST! HE...HE SAVED MY LIFE!

SAVED YOUR LIFE? THE CAPTAIN?
TELL ME HOW.
OH? UH, WELL, SURE.

I, WELL, I SORT OF MET THE CAPTAIN AT DOOGLI'S...DOOGLI MAKRIKET'S! DOOGLI, HE SELLS STUFF AT THE CRUTON MARKET, AN' CAPTAIN WAS LOOKING FOR SUPPLIES FOR THE MISSION, SEE?

ME, WELL, I WAS SORT OF IN A CAGE, YOU KNOW?

WHAT'S WITH HER IN THE CAGE?

YOU DON'T WANT THIS ONE. SHE'S A WICKED ONE... I TEACH HER FOR WRONGIN' DOOGLI MAKRIKET!

I'LL BUY HER FROM YOU.

SO CAPTAIN SPENT MOST OF HIS METAL PIECES ON ME... IF HE DIDN'T, DOOGLI WOULDA MADE A STEW OF ME—MAKE SUPPER FOR HIS LI'L MAKRIKETS. SO SEE? HE SAVED ME!
HMMM.

HOW DID YOU GET IN THAT SITUATION?

SOMETIMES YOU GET TROUBLE, SOMETIMES TROUBLE GETS YOU.

SO WITH THIS PURCHASE YOU ARE INDENTURED TO HIM?

NO. HE, LIKE, GAVE ME MY FREEDOM.
SEE? DESPITE YOUR PREJUDICE, QUIRK IS A GOOD CAPTAIN AND A FINE INDIVIDUAL. IF YOU JUDGE HIM WRONGLY, KELDORN MIGHT SEE FIT TO DO THE SAME TO YOU.

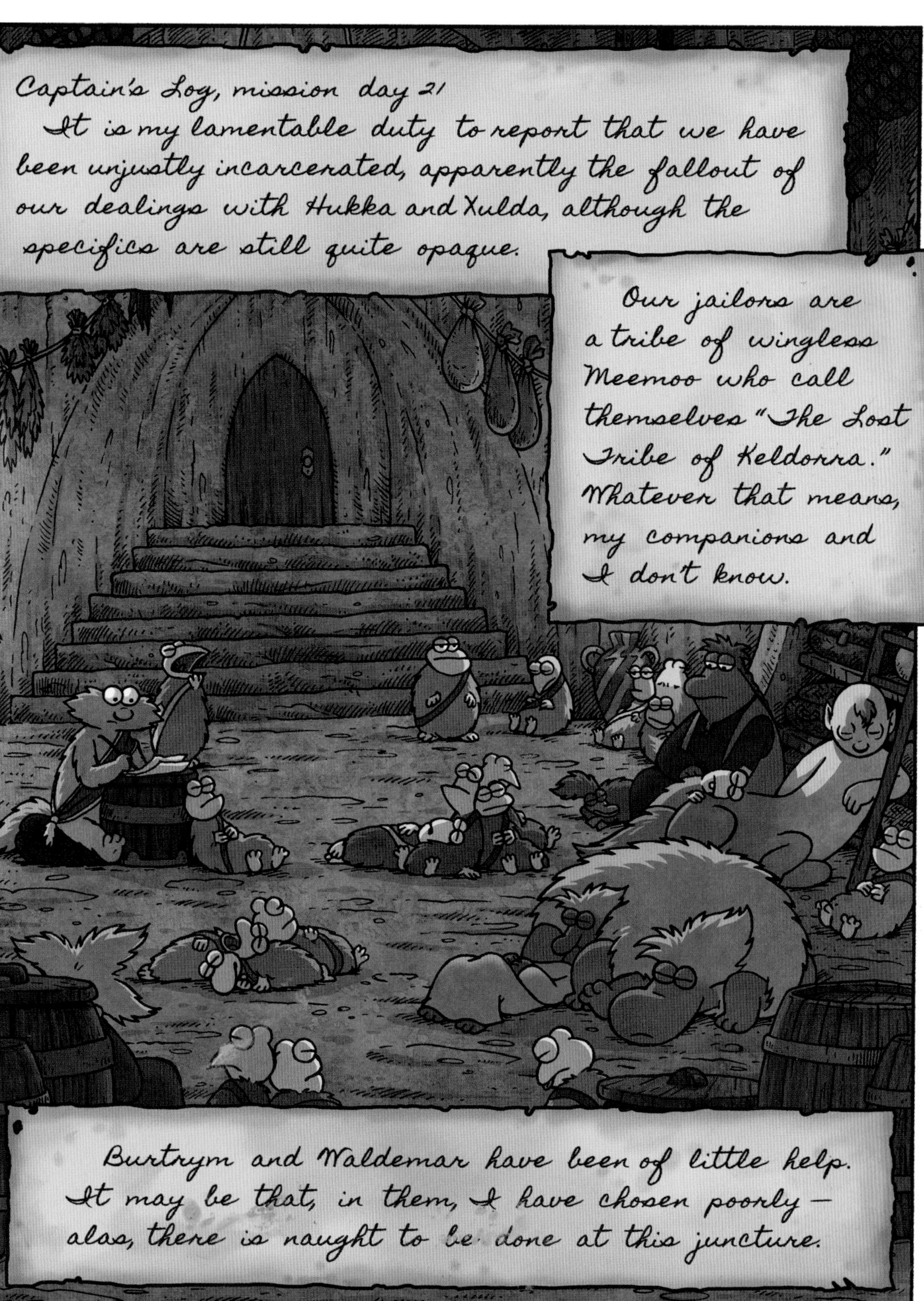
Captain's Log, mission day 21
It is my lamentable duty to report that we have been unjustly incarcerated, apparently the fallout of our dealings with Hukka and Xulda, although the specifics are still quite opaque.
Our jailors are a tribe of wingless Meemoo who call themselves "The Lost Tribe of Keldorra." Whatever that means, my companions and I don't know.
Burtrym and Waldemar have been of little help. It may be that, in them, I have chosen poorly— alas, there is naught to be done at this juncture.

Lanitee alone has knowledge of these folk, and taken away before I could learn anything of use from her... I hope she is safe! I have been promised an audience with the Matriarch of the tribe, and it is upon this meeting that I now await...

CAPTAIN, THE MATRIARCH WILL SEE YOU NOW. COME WITH US.

FINALLY! CLEUS, BURTRYM, SMOK—ACCOMPANY ME.
CAPTAIN! I CAN'T LEAVE WALDEMAR!

GADS! ALL RIGHT, THEN... SMOK, YOU STAY WITH THE GROUP.

AND SMOK, I PUT MY FULL TRUST IN YOU TO KEEP THINGS CALM AND IN ORDER.

YESSIR!

SIGH.

SO, CAPTAIN, I TRUST YOU AND YOUR COMPANIONS ARE REASONABLY COMFORTABLE.

COMFORTABLE? WE'RE PRISONERS!

I DEMAND TO KNOW WHY EMISSARIES OF THE CROWN ARE BEING TREATED LIKE CRIMINALS! IT IS OUTRAGEOUS!

CALM DOWN, CAPTAIN. WE WILL TELL YOU AS MUCH AS YOU NEED TO KNOW.

I AM TAKLAKA, KEEPER OF THE SACRED STORY-SONGS.

WE KELDORRANS HAVE GONE TO GREAT LENGTHS TO KEEP OUR WHEREABOUTS A SECRET— FOLLOWING THE WILL OF KELDORN.

WE WAIT AND READ THE OMENS, PRAYING FOR THE TIME WHEN OUR TRANSGRESSIONS ARE FORGIVEN AND OUR WINGS ARE RETURNED TO US.

ONLY WHEN WE ARE WORTHY WILL WE EMERGE FROM ISOLATION.

BUT SURELY YOUR TRIBAL AFFAIRS ARE NO CONCERN OF OURS. AND IT HARDLY WARRANTS TAKING US PRISONER.

AH, BUT IT DID, YOU SEE... EVEN THE KNOWLEDGE OF OUR WHERE-ABOUTS DEEMED IT NECESSARY.

WHAT?! THIS IS ABSURD! IF YOU HADN'T ATTACKED US WE NEVER WOULD HAVE KNOWN YOU WERE HERE!

NOT ACCORDING TO HUKKA. SHE SAID...

HUKKA?
STAND BACK!

YOU ***CAN'T*** BELIEVE HUKKA! SHE'S ***RAVING MAD!*** SHE EVEN ATTACKED HER OWN SISTER! JUST ASK XULDA.

AND WHAT EXACTLY ***DID*** XULDA TELL YOU?

MATRIARCH, IT IS TIME TO READ THE DAY'S OMENS. WE MUST GO.

ENOUGH TIME WASTED HERE.

WELL DONE, CAPTAIN.

SHUT UP, BURTRYM.

GOOD MORNING, PRIESTESS LANITEE... DID YOU SLEEP WELL?
NOT PARTICULARLY.

I AM MOST SORRY TO HEAR THAT. THE SUNS WILL BE UP SOON—WE MUST CHECK THE MORNING OMENS. WOULD YOU CARE TO JOIN US?

SURE. WHY NOT? COME ALONG, GIMIL.

SEER KESTA-NA, I HAVE BEEN THINKING... THE STORY OF YOUR TRIBE IS A VERY OLD ONE. MOST WHO KNOW IT BELIEVE IT TO BE NOTHING MORE THAN A FABLE.

A TALE TO SCARE THE FAITHLESS INTO SUBMISSION.
IT IS MUCH MORE THAN THAT. IT IS THE TRUTH.

MIGHTY KELDORN'S WRATH IS FEARSOME AND HIS JUDGMENT FINAL. WE LIVE IN ITS SHADOW EVERY DAY. SURELY YOU UNDERSTAND THIS.

I KNOW THE LEGEND, AND YET I AM SURPRISED TO FIND ANY TRUTH IN IT AT ALL.

BE CAREFUL, PRIESTESS... I RESPECT YOU, BUT YOU SHOULDN'T PUSH ME.

ANOTHER QUESTION THEN?
YES?

HUKKA AND XULDA. WHAT IS THEIR RELATION TO THE TRIBE?

THE SISTERS? AH, YES. YOUR QUESTION WOULD BE BEST ANSWERED BY TAKLAKA, THE KEEPER OF THE SACRED STORY-SONGS.

HOWEVER, I WILL ANSWER AS BEST I CAN.

ACTUALLY, THERE ARE THREE SISTERS. THEY WERE BORN OF A UNION BETWEEN A YOUNG KELDORRAN NAMED YOOKL AND THE BLARGOR XAXTROMONAX, A POWERFUL SAGE WHO HAS ADVISED US IN TIMES OF NEED...
AS YOU CAN IMAGINE, THIS UNION AND ITS OFFSPRING WAS SEEN AS A CORRUPTION OF OUR WAYS AND COULD ONLY MEAN TROUBLE FOR A TRIBE IN SEARCH OF REDEMPTION.
SO THEY WERE SENT AWAY, BANISHED FROM THE SACRED MOUNTAIN.
IT WOULD BE MANY TURNS OF THE SEASONS BEFORE WE HEARD FROM ANY OF THEM AGAIN...
ONE NIGHT IN THE FIFTH MOON OF THE COOLINGTIDE, HUKKA APPEARED, SEEKING ASYLUM. SHE WAS VERY FRIGHTENED AND CONFUSED.
ALTHOUGH WE COULD HARDLY UNDERSTAND HER, SHE WAS A DAUGHTER OF THE TRIBE SO WE TOOK HER IN....

POOR HUKKA! SHE WAS TERRIBLY SHAKEN, YET SHE WOULD NOT TELL US WHAT HAD HAPPENED TO HER.
WE NURSED HER AS BEST WE COULD, AND BY THE RISE OF THE NEXT THIRD MOON SHE SEEMED ALMOST WELL.

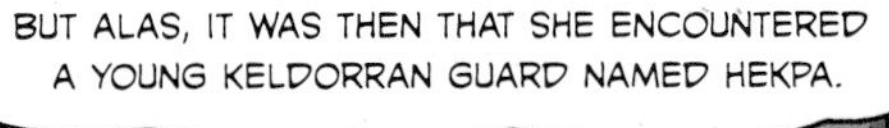
BUT ALAS, IT WAS THEN THAT SHE ENCOUNTERED A YOUNG KELDORRAN GUARD NAMED HEKPA.

HEKPA?

YES, WHY? WHAT DO YOU KNOW OF HIM?

SMOKES! IT'S JUST THAT HUKKA KEPT CALLING OUR MEEMOO SCOUT BY THAT NAME.

EL-HET-HET-WETEN'S WHISKERS! WHAT SORT OF TRICKERY IS THIS?

NO TRICKERY—IT'S TRUE. YOU MUST TELL ME WHAT HAPPENED BETWEEN HUKKA AND HEKPA! WHAT DOES IT MEAN?

I AM NOT SURE, BUT IT CAN'T BE GOOD. IT IS A QUESTION TO PUT TO THE SISTERS. THE MATRIARCH WILL BE MOST INTERESTED, THOUGH.

WHAT IS IT THAT WOULD INTEREST ME SO, KESTA-NA?

THEY KNOW OF HEKPA.

IMPOSSIBLE! THIS MUST RUN DEEPER THAN WE THOUGHT.

WE REALLY DO NOT KNOW ANYTHING OF THIS MATTER.
XULDA TOLD THEM TOO MUCH.

NO! I TELL YOU—

HMM. WELL, TO THE MATTER AT HAND... KESTA-NA, WHAT DO THE ELEMENTS TELL US?

FOG AND RAIN. GREAT KELDORN AND EL-HET-HET-WETEN ARE COLLUDING... SPREADING MISERY AND CONFUSION THIS DAY.

AND THAT GREAT DARK CLOUD?

KELDORN'S DARK FORTRESS. CHYZYKARA HAS LEFT THE DECISION UP TO HIM.

THIS IS RUBBISH! CLOUDS AND RAIN? THESE AREN'T OMENS!

THEY ARE CLEAR ENOUGH TO ME.

I AGREE. I AM BUT A HUMBLE MATRIARCH, FIT ONLY TO CARRY OUT MIGHTY KELDORN'S WHIMS.

ARE WE ALL AGREED, THEN?

AGREED.

THIS IS LUDICROUS!

OF COURSE, PRIESTESS LANITEE, ***YOU*** SHALL BE OUR HONORED GUEST INDEFINITELY.

GUARDS, ESCORT HER TO CAPTAIN KORAZON'S CHAMBER. TAKE THE LITTLE ONE BACK TO THE ROOT CELLAR AND MEET US IN MY CHAMBERS.

YOU WILL BE SAFE HERE, PRIESTESS. CAPTAIN KORAZON WILL MAKE SURE YOU ARE COMFORTABLE.

BACK TO THE CELLAR WITH YOU, LITTLE ONE.

HEY!
PRIESTESS LANITEE?

ZAIFER! HOW ARE YOU FEELING?
MOSTLY BETTER. JUST TIRED.

PRIESTESS! WELCOME.

SO THIS IS THE ZEEP PRIESTESS... WHAT IS YOUR NAME?

NEVER MIND MY NAME. I HAVE TO WARN MY COMPANIONS!

IT IS TOO LATE FOR THEM... TODAY THE TRIBUNE WILL PASS JUDGMENT FOR THE CRIMES AGAINST ZAIFER HERE.

CRIMES AGAINST ME? WHAT DO YOU MEAN?

HUKKA TOLD US WHAT YOUR CAPTAIN AND HIS FELLOWS DID TO YOUR WINGS.

UNFORGIVABLE.

HUKKA?! HUKKA'S JEEBISH AS A MELON! IT WAS SHE WHO TRIED TO CHEW MY WINGS OFF!

WHAT?! BUT THEN—
YOUR TRIBE'S LEADERS, I'M AFRAID TO SAY, MEAN TO HARM US UNDER FALSE PRETENSES.

THIS IS NOT RIGHT.
STAY HERE.

WE HAVE TO SEE THE MATRIARCH RIGHT AWAY. PYNCHYN WILL KEEP WATCH.

PLEASE! I HAVE TO GO TO MY CAPTAIN! MY COLLEAGUES...THEY ARE IN GRAVE, HORRID DANGER!

WHO AM I TO KEEP YOU HERE?

REALLY?

I DON'T WISH TO BE KEPT A PRISONER ANY MORE THAN YOU.

I WOULDN'T DARE TELL A TRUE PRIESTESS OR ONE OF THE BLESSED WHAT THEY SHOULD OR SHOULDN'T DO.

MEANWHILE...

XULDA?

HELLO?

XULDA?

XULDA!

WAIT... YOU'RE NOT XULDA.

WHAT ARE YOU DOING?

AAAAHHHH!!

HEY!

STOP HER!

GET BACK
HERE!

VILLAINS! BETRAYERS!

LEAVE ME BE, XULDA! HUKKA NO LONGER HEARS YOUR WORDS OF TREACHERY!

PLEASE, HUKKA...YOU MUST LISTEN TO ME.

TRICKERY! WHERE IS HEKPA? ***WHERE?!***

I KNOW THEY HAVE MY HEKPA!
NO!

OH, HUKKA...I AM SO SORRY, BUT HEKPA'S NOT HERE.
HEKPA'S GONE.

YOU LIE, XULDA, BUT HUKKA KNOWS THE TRUE DECIEVER...

MATRIARCH.

KESTA-NA, GO AND PREPARE THE ALTARS. I WANT THIS DONE SWIFTLY.

CAPTAIN, WE ARE BACK... THE OMENS ARE CLEAR.

GOOD. PERHAPS WE CAN PROCEED AS CIVILIZED CRUTONIAN CITIZENS. DID YOU SPEAK WITH XULDA?

WAIT! WHAT'S GOING ON?

CAPTAIN, IT IS OUT OF OUR HANDS. IT IS KELDORN'S WILL. OUR TRIBE MUST REMAIN HIDDEN UNTIL OUR SIN IS CLEANSED.

WHEN THE KING LEARNS THAT I AM MISSING, THERE WILL BE SEVERE REPERCUSSIONS!

WE WILL DEAL WITH THAT PROBLEM IF AND WHEN IT ARISES.

WE ARE BUT HUMBLE SERVANTS OF KELDORN. WE WILL CARRY OUT HIS WILL AS SWIFTLY AND PAINLESSLY AS POSSIBLE.
PLEASE! YOU DON'T NEED TO HARM THE CAPTAIN!

YOU MISUNDERSTAND. YOU MUST ALL BE SILENCED.

SILENCED, MATRIARCH?

HUKKA! WHAT ARE YOU DOING HERE?
YOU MUST OBEY THE LAWS OF KELDORRA. GO BACK TO YOUR ROOM.

KELDORRA? KELDORRA GIVES HEKPA, KELDORRA TAKES HEKPA...

HUKKA HATES KELDORRA!!
ZORCH!

CHYZYKARA'S EYE SEES ALL, AND KELDORN WILL PUNISH YOU AGAIN FOR THIS!

KELDORN TAKES SWEET HEKPA! MATRIARCH TAKES HUKKA'S HEKPA!!

WHERE IS MY HEKPA? WHERE?!
ZOMPH!

ACH!

RRRRRRRRRRRRRRRR

ZORCH!

HEKPAAAAAA...

MATRIARCH! SHE'S...DEAD!

QUIRK! THIS IS ALL YOUR FAULT! YOU SHOULD NOT HAVE COME HERE.

GUARDS. YOU ARE MY WITNESSES... QUIRK AND HIS COMPANIONS CAUSED THE DEATH OF OUR MATRIARCH AND HUKKA. THEY MUST DIE. KELDORN DEMANDS IT.

AAH!

OOF!

THWAK
KEEPER OF THE SACRED STORY-SONGS, WE MUST GET YOU TO SAFETY.

BONK

WALDEMAR, QUICK! GET ON MY BACK!

HURRY!
DONK
OUTTA THE WAY!!

YOWP!

DONK

UK...

BURTRYM! ARE YOU ALL RIGHT?
OOOG

ALAS, I AM DONE FOR... LEAVE ME AND SAVE YOURSELVES, BUT PLEASE...
...TAKE CARE OF WALDEMAR...

YOWCH!!

LOOKS FINE.
HRUMPH! WATCH IT, YOU!

LET'S GET OUT OF HERE QUICK, BEFORE MORE GUARDS SHOW UP!

OW! OW! OW! OW! OW!

HUKKA?

OH, HUKKA!

QUICKLY! THIS WAY!

...NOT ONLY THAT, BUT THEY KILLED THE MATRIARCH, TOO!

OOP!

HALT, VILLAINS!

KELDORN WILL FEED ON YOUR SOULS!

WE'VE GOT TO GET YOU OUT OF HERE.
NOW!

GIMIL!

WHAT'S HAPPENING? HAVE YOU SEEN ANY OF THE OTHERS? QUIRK?

UM, UH...YEAH. THE CAPTAIN AND A BUNCH...THEY ESCAPED, BUT I THINK, UH, THE OTHERS ARE STILL IN THE CELLAR AND STUFF.

SMOKES! WE MUST FREE THEM! DO YOU REMEMBER HOW TO GET BACK TO THE CELLAR?
I THINK SO.

XULDA! IT'S HUKKA—SHE...

I KNOW, DEAR...I KNOW. THERE IS NOTHING TO BE DONE NOW BUT SAVE OURSELVES. QUICK! THIS WAY!

UH-OH.
XULDA! WHAT NEW TREACHERY IS THIS?

STAND ASIDE, TAKLAKA. THIS HAS ALL GONE TOO FAR.

YOU DO REALIZE THAT THESE INTRUDERS KILLED ***BOTH*** THE MATRIARCH ***AND*** YOUR SISTER?

I WOULD HAVE EXPECTED THE KEEPER OF THE SACRED STORY-SONGS TO HAVE HER FACTS STRAIGHT.

IT'S YOUR SUPERSTITION THAT HAS CAUSED ALL OF THIS SUFFERING... YOURS AND NOW MINE! STAND ASIDE OR I WILL MAKE YOU.

GASP
ZUPPA!

MAY ZNX SPARE US ALL!

WHO IS RESPONSIBLE FOR SLAUGHTERING MY SISTER HUKKA?

WHO?!

ZUPPA! IT WAS THE OUTSIDERS! THEY HAVE INFILTRATED OUR HOME AND KILLED HUKKA!

I THINK PERHAPS NOT.

NO, ZUPPA!
REDEEM YOURSELF IN THE EYES OF KELDORN!!

ZUPPA! NO!!
BLAM!

HMMMM...

SO, DEAR SISTER, WHAT'S THIS MESS YOU'VE GOTTEN US INTO?

MOST INTERESTING.

YOU REALLY SHOULD SHARE YOUR PLAYTHINGS.
ZOOMPH!

NO!

HA HA HA HA HA HA HA HA!

OH, XULDA, YOU ALWAYS WERE THE WEAK ONE.

NOW, WHERE WAS I?

ZUPPA! BE REASONABLE!

REASONABLE?
WAS IT REASONABLE FOR YOU TO BANISH MY PARENTS?

ZORCH!

WAS IT REASONABLE FOR YOU TO MURDER MY SISTER?

ZORCH!

WAS IT REASONABLE FOR YOU TO DENY ME MY BIRTHRIGHT?
PLEASE, NO!

NO, TAKLAKA...
...THE TIME FOR BEING REASONABLE IS OVER.

ZORCH!

BLAM!
HA HA HA HA HA HA HA HA!
BLAM!

BLAM!

KKKKKKKKKKKKKCH
KHHHAATHOOOOMM!!

BURTRYM, WE HAVE TO GET OUT OF HERE!

WALDEMAR...

THERE IS NOTHING WE CAN DO FOR WALDEMAR—OR FOR CLEUS. THEY'RE JUST NOT HERE.

PULL IT TOGETHER, CHAP! WE CAN ONLY SAVE OURSELVES!

KATHOOOMM!!

...AND THAT'S WHY YOU NEVER WALK BEHIND A BLADDERWAGGON.

QUICK! EVERYONE OUT!

WHAT, ALREADY?

QUICKLY NOW!

FOLLOW GIMIL. EVERYONE HURRY!

KATHOOOMM!!

Characters of Note

CAPTAIN QUENTERINDY QUIRK
CAPTAIN, MISSION LEADER

NERSEL BUKUBAY
CARTOGRAPHER ROYAL

BURTRYM
ECOLOGIST

WALDEMAR
ECOLOGIST

SMOK
QUIRK'S ASSISTANT

ARKARK
SMOK'S PET

LANITEE
BOTANIST
(PRIESTESS/HEALER)

CLEUS
LANITEE'S APPRENTICE

GIMIL
SCOUT

ZAIFER
SCOUT

SORRILLIUS
CHEF

HUKKA
RECLUSE/SORCERESS

XULDA
WEAVER/SORCERESS

ZUPPA
SORCERESS

XAXTROMONAX
SAGE

YOOKL

Map of the Upper Mabooglaqui Valley
by Nersel Bukubay, Cartographer Royal

N
W
E
S
Lukki's Grotto
Hukka's Caves
Base Camp
Roxxann Cage
Xulda's House
Mabooglaqui River
Mount Keldorra

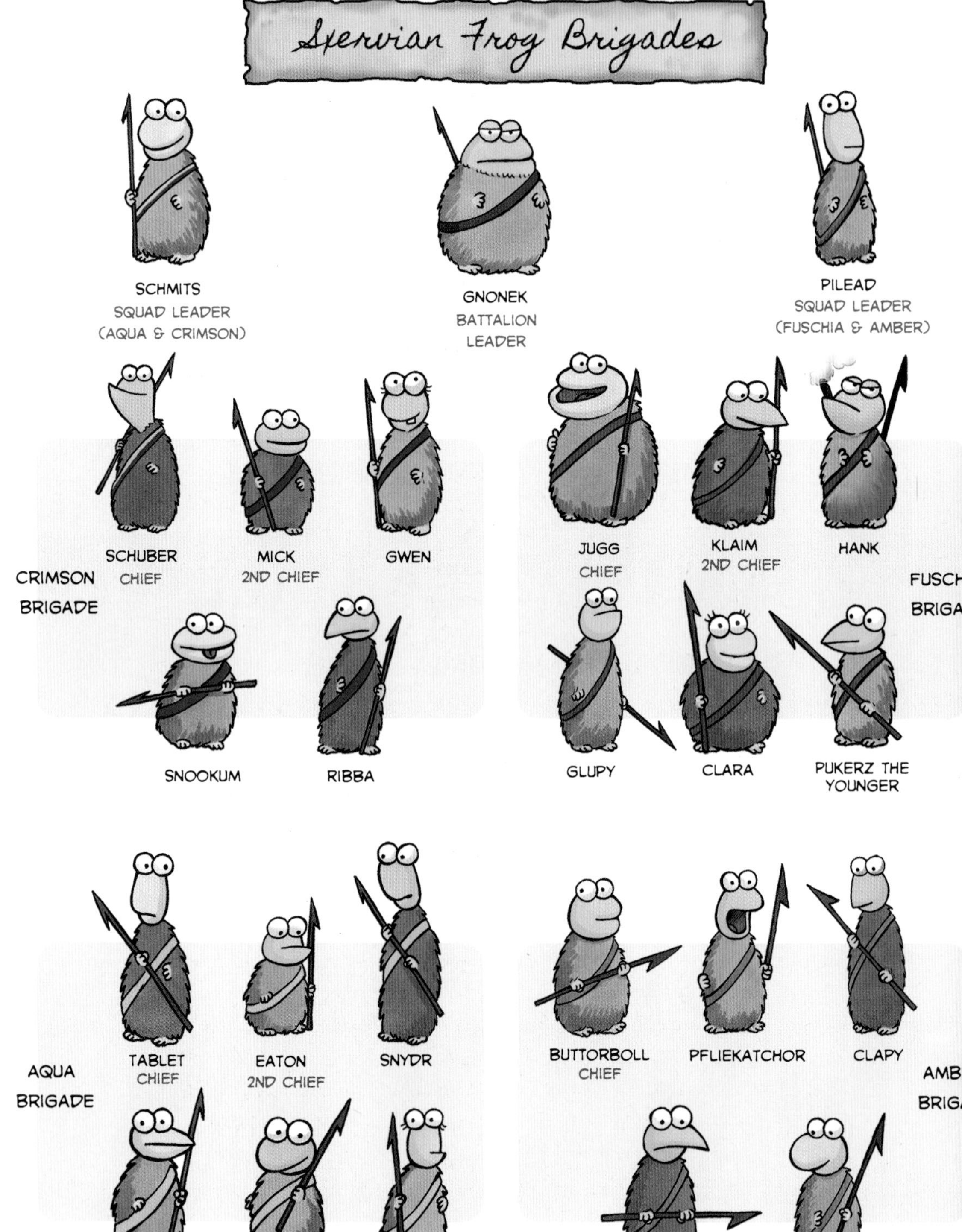

Sxervian Frog Brigades
SCHMITS
SQUAD LEADER
(AQUA & CRIMSON)
GNONEK
BATTALION
LEADER
PILEAD
SQUAD LEADER
(FUSCHIA & AMBER)
CRIMSON
BRIGADE
SCHUBER
CHIEF
MICK
2ND CHIEF
GWEN
SNOOKUM
RIBBA
JUGG
CHIEF
KLAIM
2ND CHIEF
HANK
GLUPY
CLARA
PUKERZ THE
YOUNGER
AQUA
BRIGADE
TABLET
CHIEF
EATON
2ND CHIEF
SNYDR
PUKERZ THE
ELDER
CLARK
BETH
BUTTORBOLL
CHIEF
PFLIEKATCHOR
CLAPY
PERIKETE
GURNEY

Robert Christie grew up on Long Island where he spent most of his waking hours obsessively drawing anything and everything, except cars. While taking cover from a lunchroom food fight, he met Deborah Lang, and shortly thereafter they conspired to create Crutonia. Ever since, they have been writing stories set in their quirky made-up world. After earning his BFA in St. Louis, he moved to Jersey City where he makes his living as an illustrator, painter, and prop maker for major motion pictures, Broadway, and fashion photo shoots. He has been writing and further developing Crutonia with Deborah for more than three decades, and is so grateful to be able to share it with you all in the Quirk's Quest series.

Deborah Lang is a cartoonist, scientific illustrator, and molecular biologist. She was born in New York City but eventually moved to Long Island purely to meet up with Rob Christie to create Crutonia. In addition to the Quirk's Quest series, she has published drawings and stories in newspapers, international science journals, anthologies through the Let's Make Comics collective in Chicago, and several Crutonia comic books with her collaborator, Rob. In 2017, Deborah moved to Boston to join the faculty of Boston University as a cancer biologist.

Acknowledgments

We are so grateful to so many people for their support. Although there is not enough space here to list everyone, we would like to highlight the following people: The Andys, Kim Fudge, Margie Fair, our nieces and nephews (Annalise, Jeb, Meredith, Eli, Noah, Celia, Zach, Caroline, Abram, and Vincent), Melissa Sayen and the rest of our colleagues at Let's Make Comics Chicago, and especially the wonderful crew at First Second: Chris Duffy, Robyn Chapman, Gina Gagliano, Danielle Ceccolini, and Mark Siegel. Thank you for making all of this possible!